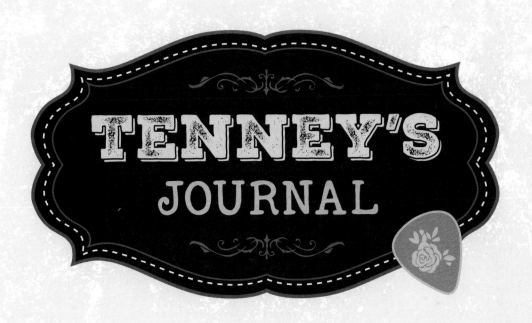

★ American Girl®

TENNEY'S JOURNAL

Scholastic Inc.

J
Series
AMERICAN
TENNEY

Text by Molly Hodgin, based on the stories in *Tenney* and *Tenney in the Key of Friendship* by Kellen Hertz • "Star Like Me" and "April Springs" lyrics by Kellen Hertz • "Reach the Sky" music and lyrics by Leah Bryan and Hannah Fisher • "Where You Are" music and lyrics by Ashley Leone • "Music in Me" lyrics by Kate Cosentino • Doodles and artwork by Dirty Bandits • Photos of Jaya by Michael Frost • Digital photo illustrations of Tenney, Logan, and Jaya by Juliana Kolesova

Cover design by Angela Jun and Becky James • Interior design by Carla Alpert

Images ©: page 8: Olena Brodetska/Shutterstock, Inc.; page 9: Maria Kazanova/iStockphoto; page 11: JDawnInk/iStockphoto; page 15: Richard Ellis/Alamy Images; page 16: David S. Baker/Shutterstock, Inc.; page 29: Kano07/Shutterstock, Inc.; page 42: NEGOVURA/Shutterstock, Inc.; page 45: Paul Briden/Alamy Images; page 55: Radharc Images/Alamy Images; page 63: kridsada tipchot/Shutterstock, Inc.; page 69: Stacey Oldham/iStockphoto; page 72: topform84/iStockphoto; page 88: Alex Tihonovs/Shutterstock, Inc.; page 110: Mamunur Rashid/Alamy Images; page 135: Mamunur Rashid/Alamy Images; page 149 top: JonnyDrake/Shutterstock, Inc.; page 149 bottom: michelangeloop/Shutterstock, Inc.

americangirl.com/service

ISBN 978-1-338-13704-0
10 9 8 7 6 5 4 3 2 1   17 18 19 20 21
Printed in the U.S.A. 23 • First printing 2017

Attention: An adult's involvement is needed for some or all of the recipes in this book. Check ingredients lists for allergies.

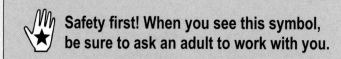

Safety first! When you see this symbol,
be sure to ask an adult to work with you.

THIS JOURNAL
Belongs To:

Tennyson Evangeline Grant,
a.k.a. Tenney

ALL for Y'ALL

Dear Tenney,

Happy Birthday! I'm so proud of the budding musician you've become. Every songwriter needs a place to write down her ideas—I thought maybe this could be yours.

Love,
Mom (and Dad)

ALL ABOUT ME

NAME: Tennyson Grant

HOMETOWN: Nashville, Tennessee

SCHOOL: Magnolia Hills ~~Elementary~~ Middle School

PARENTS: Georgia and Ray Grant

SIBLINGS: Mason and Aubrey

PETS: Waylon, a golden retriever

BFF: Jaya Mitra

HOBBIES: Playing guitar, ^and banjo singing, writing songs, cooking with my mom

DREAMS: To share my songs with the world!

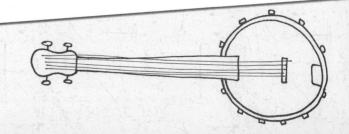

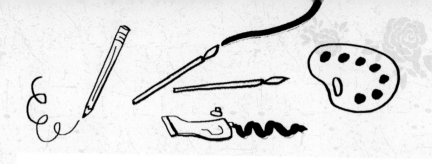

MY BFF

NAME: Jaya Mitra

HOMETOWN: Nashville, Tennessee

SCHOOL: Magnolia Hills ~~Elementary~~ Middle School

BEST QUALITIES: Creative, kind, generous, compassionate

FAVORITE THINGS: Art supplies, rainbows, pancakes, and videos of puppies and piglets!

SILLIEST QUOTE: Well butter my butt and call me a biscuit! 😋

HAPPY PLACE: The art room at school

CRANK UP THE CONFIDENCE

Monday, May 9th

Guess What?

Dad let me perform onstage with the Tri-Stars today! He says I've got a long way to go with my guitar playing, but everybody's got to start performing somewhere, sometime, and it's only right my first performance be with the family band. I just played one song, and you could hardly even hear me under Dad's guitar, but still—it was amazing! I can't wait until I can get up there again.

 Like 1

 ▶ MP3 ✉ Email 🖨 Print

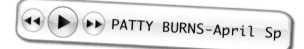

◀◀ ▶ ▶▶ PATTY BURNS-April Sp

PATTY BURNS LYRICS

 ## Play "April Springs"...

"APRIL SPRINGS"
Last April the rains came down,
And washed away your love.

Last April the rains came down,
and washed away my pride.

When I lost your heart in that rainstorm,
I think I nearly died.

Waylon's Song

I've got a best bud

He likes to roll in the mud

~~He looks like a bear~~ He's wild and he's crazy

~~When I pet his soft golden hair~~

But mostly he's lazy

Oh, Waylon

Wayyy-lon!

I ♥ Waylon!

Oh, Waylon

Wayyy-lon!

He's a real sweet pooch

Long as you make sure

He's not on the loose

Wayyy-lon!

Always sniffing for food,

He's a furry little dude

If you aren't quick

He'll give you a lick

Oh, Waylon

Wayyy-lon!

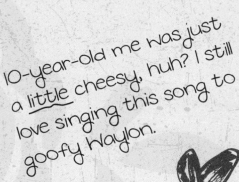

10-year-old me was just a little cheesy, huh? I still love singing this song to goofy Waylon.

Oh, Waylon

Wayyy-lon!

He's a real sweet pooch

Long as you make sure

He's not on the loose

Wayyy-lon!

Nashville's Best
Concert Venues

I need to see shows at ALL of them!

Grand Ole Opry ✓
Ryman Auditorium ✓
Bridgestone Arena
Bluebird Cafe ✓
3rd and Lindsley ✓
Mercy Lounge
Centennial Park and the Parthenon ✓
Exit/In
Cannery Ballroom ✓
Station Inn
12th & Porter
Tennessee Performing Arts Center ✓
Schermerhorn Symphony Center ✓
Wildhorse Saloon

LIVE
ENTERTAINMENT
SATURDAY
JULY 20
GRAND
OLE OPRY

Seat   Section   Row
20   01   01
NO REFUNDS $20

LIVE MUSIC
CONCERT
★ WITH SPECIAL GUESTS

Tennessee
Performing Arts
Center

SATURDAY, AUGUST 1

DOORS OPEN AT 7:00 P.M.
ALL AGES EVENT

41	B	22
Seat	Section	Row

LOUD   ROCK
LIVE CONCERT
MUSICAL   GUESTS

RYMAN
AUDITORIUM 8/10

DOORS OPEN AT 7:00 P.M.
ALL AGES EVENT

2	1	1
Seat	Section	Row

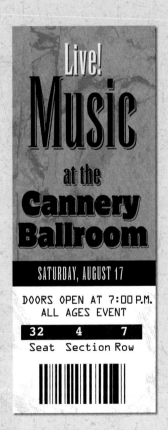

Live!
Music
at the
Cannery
Ballroom

SATURDAY, AUGUST 17

DOORS OPEN AT 7:00 P.M.
ALL AGES EVENT

32	4	7
Seat	Section	Row

Rework for
Mockingbird showcase?

Home Again

The highway signs are rollin' by
And the sun is sinking low
But I can't stop or ~~turn around~~ slow down
Because there's not much ~~further~~ more to go
Until I'm home again

Nashville's lights are bright tonight
Shining out across the river
~~Strains of music fill the breeze~~ Music fills the
The beauty makes me shiver   evening air

I'm home again, finally home again
Home sweet Tennessee
I'm home again, finally home again
There's nowhere else I'd rather be
Than home again

The world is such a big, huge place
I want to ~~travel everywhere~~ roam and see it all
~~Wonders and sights~~   ← The view just takes
And soon it's easy to feel small my breath away
Until I'm home again

I'm home again, finally home again
Home sweet Tennessee
I'm home again, finally home again
There's nowhere else I'd rather be
Than home again

If I ever feel I've lost my way
Been knocked ~~down on my back~~ way off of track
~~Home is my true north~~ Home will call out my name

And I can always make it ~~home~~ back

Back home again

I'm home again, finally home again
Home sweet Tennessee
I'm home again, finally home again
There's nowhere else I'd rather be
Than home again

Saturday, October 1st

Things are starting to feel different when it comes to me and my music . . . it's hard to describe. Maybe writing in here will help me "process things," as Mom always says . . .

••• ———————— •••• ———————— •••

I've been thinking about our Tri-Stars rehearsal today. We only got through 3 songs before Jesse called it quits to take a phone call. How are we supposed to get better as a band if the lead singer just leaves in the middle of rehearsal?! (I definitely know that if I were the lead singer, I would NEVER do that to my band!!!) And the Tri-Stars gave Jesse her start in Nashville. The only reason she gets solo gigs now and then is because people saw her perform with the Tri-Stars. (I mean, maybe her phone call was a family emergency or something, but does answering "Not much. Just here with the band" seem like the start of an emergency call? I think not.) Walking out in the middle of rehearsal is SO not professional!

I guess if I'm being totally honest, Jesse frustrates me so much because I do secretly want to sing lead someday. Here she is with the chance to do what she loves and she doesn't even take it seriously. I just don't get it.

I bet when I'm a little bit older Dad will let me take the lead on a few songs and perform some of the songs I've written with the Tri-Stars. That would be awesome!

ALL for Y'ALL

I BELIEVE IN NASHVILLE

Love seeing these "I believe in Nashville" murals around town!

Still October 1st!

I'm not the biggest Belle Starr fan, but I have to admit it was pretty cool to hear her play live tonight in Centennial Park, even if Aubrey was kinda hyper about it! I guess I'd be pretty pumped if I got a chance to see my favorite singer live.

It was nice to spend time with Mom helping out in the food truck, too. I love watching her cook and I love tasting what she makes even more! She's the best cook I know—and I think it's because she loves it so much. When she's working on a new recipe, she gets in that zone like I do when I'm songwriting, or how I've seen Jaya when she's designing something. It's nice to see Mom shine like that.

I will always be in awe of the Parthenon in Centennial Park!

Star Like Me, by Belle Star

Look in the mirror and love what you see.
Seek and discover who you can be.
Be proud of yourself like I am of me.
Know who you are and you'll be free.

You can be a star like me!
If you follow your dream,
you'll be a star like me!

Okay . . . I admit it—Belle's lyrics <u>are</u> really catchy! And she's right—I want to be a star and I've know I've got it in me, but I also want to be ME. Sometimes I worry I can't be both . . .

P.S. It's the next morning and Belle Starr's lyrics are STILL stuck in my head!!! Ugh.

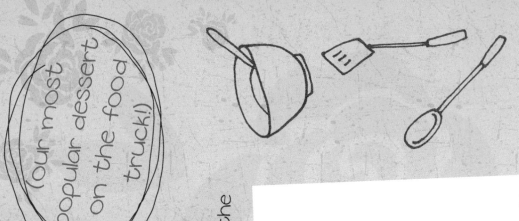

(our most popular dessert on the food truck!)

GEORGIA'S
CRISPY-GOOEY-CRUNCHY BARS

Have to remember to use oven mitts so I don't burn my hands, and a trivet or pot holder so I don't burn the counter!

THE CRISPY

Spray a 9 x 13-inch pan with cooking spray. In a large saucepan, **melt 2 tablespoons of butter** over low heat. Add **4 cups of mini marshmallows** and stir until completely melted. Take pan off heat.

Add **6 cups crispy rice cereal** and stir until completely coated, then pour into the 9 x 13 pan. Spray spatula with cooking spray and use it to press mixture evenly in pan. Let this layer cool on the countertop or in the fridge.

Reminder to self: Do not touch mixture with my hands—it's very hot!

THE GOOEY

In a medium saucepan, heat **12 ounces of milk chocolate chips** and **1 can of sweetened condensed milk**, stirring constantly, until the chocolate chips are melted. Pour "goo" over the cool crispy layer and spread evenly.

Marshmallows aren't technically crunchy, but . . . oh well!

THE CRUNCHY

Sprinkle **2 cups of dry roasted peanuts** and **2 cups of mini marshmallows** evenly over gooey layer. Put pan in fridge to cool (about 30 minutes). Cut into 24 squares and serve. Store bars on countertop or in fridge.

Enjoy the crispy-gooey-crunchy goodness in all its glory!

Monday, October 3rd

The Jamboree is still two whole months away, but I'm so excited! Last year's festival raised enough money for our school to buy a new snack cart, but this year's is going to be even better! Jaya convinced me to sign up with her to be on the Jamboree Steering Committee—should be fun! I'm also trying to decide if I should sign up to perform as one of the musical acts. I want to, but I get butterflies just thinking about singing in front of the whole school. What if I mess up?

The only thing I'm not so excited about is that Holliday Hayes won the vote for 6th grade chairperson of the committee. Jaya totally should have won (not that I'm biased or anything ☺). It seems like Holliday gets everything she wants just because her dad is a VP at Silver Sun Records and her family has a ton of money. I know Jaya was disappointed, but hopefully we can just have fun working together!

Thursday, October 6th

I was pretty nervous today when we went to the Lillian Street Senior Center. I like Ms. Carter's idea to pair us with seniors from the center to work on the Jamboree, but my partner, Portia, was pretty grouchy. It seemed like everyone else was having fun with their partners, but mine barely even answered my questions. I wonder how I can cheer her up and get her excited about the Jamboree . . . or anything at all.

Maybe this would cheer her up?

RANDOM SONG IDEA:

"Jumpin' Jamboree"

An upbeat, party song

What can Portia and I do together
for the Jamboree?

- -

* Work at the bake sale

    (make crispy-gooey-crunchy bars?)
* Set-up crew to get all the booths ready
* Clean-up crew after the Jamboree's over
* Work the ticket booth
* Help out at the cupcake-decorating booth
* Pass out maps of the booths
* Work at the make-your-own-sweet-tea booth

- -

I know all of those things need to be done,
but they just don't sound very fun. I wish
Portia and I could find something really
interesting to do. Maybe I'll see if I can get
a different partner . . .

Jaya and her partner are doing a letterpress-
printing booth—so cool! And he and Jaya are
both SO excited about their idea. Why couldn't
I have found someone enthusiastic like that?!

Lyrics Brainstorm:

This song's for you, my love
You watch over me from above
~~Who looks like a sweet white dove~~
~~Whose arms fit me like a glove?~~
~~Who gives me a big shove?~~

Ugh! Nothing good rhymes with love!

Who is my love? What is this song even about? Why can't I think of any good lyrics???

Argghhhh!!!!

Other song ideas:

* Something about that feeling you get when you know you're SO close to getting something you want SO bad, but it still seems so far away
* Something about friendship—how your best friend will be there for you no matter what
* "Never gonna give up"

Tri-Star Set List

1. "Workin' Man Blues" by Merle Haggard

2. "The Devil Went Down to Georgia" by the Charlie Daniels Band

3. "Carolina Highway" by Ray Grant (a.k.a. Dad!)

4. "Wildwood Flower" by the Carter Family

5. "April Springs" by Patty Burns

6. "Ring of Fire" by Johnny Cash

7. "She's the One" by Ray Grant

8. "It's Tennessee for Me" by Ray Grant

FRESH PICKED

Geez. I almost accidentally put "Star Like Me" by Belle Starr on here— it's been on repeat in my brain since her concert. I've got to get it out of my head!!!

Saturday, October 8th

The Tri-Stars had a gig today at East Park
for the Neighborhood Association mixer
and the most amazing thing happened!
Diva Jesse wasn't there a few minutes
before we were supposed to go onstage.
We thought maybe she was just (very!)
late, but then Dad called her and she QUIT
the band! Yikes!! Dad could sing lead on
most of the songs—but not on "Carolina
Highway" or "Wildwood Flower" since those
songs are too high for his deep voice, so
I volunteered to sing them!!! This was my
chance to sing lead, but it was so sudden
and I was REALLY nervous when I walked

RANDOM SONG IDEA:
"Waiting in the Wings"
Ballad about waiting for
your big break!

out onto that stage. I had one tiny hiccup on the first chorus, but no one noticed and I felt totally exhilarated by the end. I just love performing! Seeing the audience dancing and loving the music I was singing was amazing—it really is the BEST feeling in the whole world. And it sounds like Dad might let me sing lead on a few songs permanently! Yay! I can't wait to perform again!! It feels so good that he's proud of me. I think I'll do even better next time after actually rehearsing the lead parts!

I love our new stickers!!

Jamboree
Planning Playlist

"Shake It Off" by Taylor Swift

"Genesis" by Grimes

"Somebody Like You" by Keith Urban

"Here Comes the Sun" by the Beatles

"Chicken Fried" by Zac Brown Band

"Crocodile Rock" by Elton John

"Life in Film" by Get Closer

"Long Live" by Taylor Swift

"Saturday in the Park" by Chicago

"All Shook Up" by Elvis

Sunday, October 9th

The most AMAZING thing happened today—I was playing my new song in one of the listening rooms at Dad's store and a woman from Mockingbird Records heard me and gave me her business card! She thinks I have talent, and she invited me to come perform in a showcase at the Bluebird Cafe!

Can you believe it? THE BLUEBIRD CAFE!!! Taylor Swift was discovered at the Bluebird!! Mom and Dad are worried I might be too young, so they haven't given me permission to play yet. But they also haven't said no, so there's hope!

This could be my big break, which means
I better get to practicing! Ahhhhhhhh!!!!
I'm so excited I can barely stand it!

ALL
for
Y'ALL

MOCKINGBIRD
RECORDS

Ellie Cale
A&R Coordinator
Mockingbird Records
260 Treble Square
Nashville, TN 37203

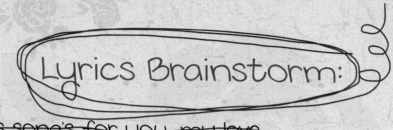

Lyrics Brainstorm:

~~This song's for you, my love~~
~~You watch over me from above~~

. . . and I can't think of anything else . . .

Is this a love song? It sounds like a love song . . . but I've definitely never been in love myself. What do people in love even feel?

I think it might be time for my Super-Secret Writer's-Block Song . . .

DO NOT EVER PLAY THIS IN PUBLIC—

To be sung only in extreme writer's-block
emergencies IN PRIVATE!!!

I've got to giggle
It makes me wiggle
And then I wriggle
All around the room
Baby, won't you giggle, too?

I've got to dance
Like I'm from France
Twist and prance
All around the room
Baby, won't you dance with me?

I've got to sing
Hit those guitar strings
Belt it like it ain't no thing
All around the room
Baby, won't you sing with me?

I know it's silly but singing it snaps me out of
the slump every time!

Monday, October 10th

So we visited the seniors at the center again for a Jamboree planning session. A few minutes in, I noticed something weird— Portia's fingers had calluses just like mine! She plays guitar, too! (And her guitar is REALLY pretty—I've never seen anything like it at Dad's shop.) I played my new song for her. It felt weird to play my brand-new song for someone I barely know, but she was really nice about it and treated me like a real songwriter and not just a kid playing guitar. I felt like I could trust her with my music. And then, before I knew it, I had told her all about the showcase and how my parents maybe thought I was too young to play. She's really easy to talk to, and she gave me some good advice. I want to write it down before I forget it!

"You need to figure out what you want to say with your music. When you know that, you'll find your voice as an artist. And that's something no one can ever take away from you."
—Portia Burns

"There's no such thing as too young in music. It's not about age; it's about being ready."
—Portia Burns

I'm really glad Portia is my partner. Finding a grown-up musician who takes me seriously (and isn't one of my parents!) is really cool.

Song Options for Bluebird Showcase:

"Home Again" Maybe?

"~~Carolina Highways~~" Dad wrote it — not me
(I'm supposed to sing one of my own songs)

"~~Good Morning Glory~~" — Too sweet

"~~Waylon's Song~~" — DEFINITELY NOT!
(sorry, Waylon!)

"To strive, to seek, to find,
and not to yield."
—Alfred, Lord Tennyson

My dad named me after Lord
Tennyson because he's always loved
Tennyson's poetry. This might sound
totally cheeseball, but whenever I feel
overwhelmed, I repeat that quote to
myself and it reminds me not to give up.

Songwriting's difficult, but my dad always
says that my songs should be <u>my</u> music
and <u>my</u> voice and <u>my</u> words. I'm going
to <u>STRIVE</u> and <u>FIND</u> the write words for
a song that will show everyone at the
Bluebird exactly who Tenney Grant is. No
<u>YIELDING</u> for this girl!!!

♫ RANDOM SONG IDEA:
"Never Give Up!"
Girl-power ballad?

Sunday, October 16th

Aaarrrgggghhh!!!!!!

My parents aren't going to let me perform at the Bluebird Showcase. They still think I'm too young to be pursuing a professional music career, but I know they're wrong. Tanya Tucker and LeAnn Rimes were both only 13 when they had their first hits, and Taylor Swift has been a professional songwriter since she was 14! 12 is a teeny-tiny bit younger, but even if I did get a record deal, it would take at least a couple of years before I'd have an album out—it's not like I'd become a megastar overnight or something (and that's not the goal anyway . . . though it might be nice). ☺ I just don't understand why they want to stand in the way of my dreams! I'm too sad to even think about singing or writing songs for a while . . .

Singer-songwriters who got their big breaks when they were young ➔

Taylor Swift
Sang at 76ers game at 11
First album at 16

That's even younger than me!

Dolly Parton
Appeared at Grand
Olde Opry at 13

Rachel Holder
Sang at LA Lakers game at 14
Released first album at 18

I'll be 13 in less than a year!

LeAnn Rimes
13 when "Blue" hit #3
on Billboard charts

Tanya Tucker
Released "Delta Dawn" when she was 13

Miranda Lambert
Performed in Johnnie High's
Country Music Revue at 16

Lennon & Maisy Stella
13 and 9 when released viral cover of
"Call Your Girlfriend"
(Love these gals so much)

TENNEY GRANT

Singer-songwriter extraordinaire

Performing one night only at Nashville's famous

BLUEBIRD CAFE!

Too bad this poster will never see the light of day. But it did make me feel better!

This flyer Jaya made is AMAZING!!! Jaya is amazing!

AMAZING

BFF

SHINE

Monday, October 17th

We went to the **Ryman Auditorium** for a field trip today. I LOVE it so much. I get chills every time I go to a concert there, thinking about all of the incredible musicians who have performed there like Johnny Cash, Dolly Parton, Patsy Cline, and even Elvis!

During the field trip, we each got to walk onstage alone and stand in the spotlight. It felt like home. Now I'm even more sure— someday I'm going to stand on that stage and sing my heart out for hundreds of people. Maybe the audience will even drum the backs of the pews (The Ryman was originally a church!) to ask me for an encore! It's my favorite Ryman tradition!

I'm not going to let anything stand in the way of making it there to perform. So what if my parents won't let me play at the Bluebird? The important thing is to keep writing great songs and perform whenever I can. And I'm going to start by performing at the Jamboree!

I WILL stand here again someday!

P.S. Belle Starr's song is back on repeat in my head, but I don't even mind it so much today! If you follow your dream, you'll be a star like me!

Goals for Getting My Music Out There:

1. Perform in public—anywhere and as much as I can!

2. Write a song that expresses who I really am

3. Perform at the Bluebird or another awesome venue (I need to go back and check my list of best venues in Nashville for more ideas!)

4. Get a manager

5. Sign a record deal!

6. Record my first album so I can share my music with the world!

Lyrics Brainstorm:

~~This song's for you, my love~~
~~You watch over me from above~~

Love, miss, night, stars

~~In the quiet still of the night~~
~~My heart grows wings and takes flight~~
~~I look for you in starless skies~~
~~To search for love in your eyes~~

My love, my love, where can you be?
Why have you gone away from me?
My love, my love, please tell me true
Is my love enough for you?

Ugh. These lyrics aren't working and they're totally the wrong rhythm anyway. Time to step back and rethink things.

Portia told me that a good song is always about something meaningful to you. This song needs to be about someone I love. But who?

I love Waylon . . . but I've already got a song about him. ☺

I love my mom—even when we don't see eye to eye. She works so hard for us and I wouldn't be who I am without her supporting me all the way. I just want to make her proud of me.

Reach the Sky
(Song for Mom)

I am planted in the ground

~~Steady as a tree~~

Tiny like a seed

~~Someday I hope you'll see~~

Someday I will make you proud

I'll be ~~sturdy~~ steady like a ~~weed~~ tree

~~Because you gave me roots~~

Will you ~~show~~ teach me how to grow?

Gonna be myself, ~~ain't no one~~ nobody else

Gonna ~~touch~~ reach the sky if I only try

I ~~know that~~ admit that I am young

~~Safe under~~ Tucked beneath your wings

~~Soon enough~~

But someday I'll be on my own

~~Singin' loud~~

Wild and flying free

~~'Cause you taught me~~ how to sing?

Will you teach me

Gonna be myself, nobody else

Gonna reach the sky if I only try

Wanna keep me

I know you ~~want me to take it slow~~

Safe away at home

But I've got ~~lots of~~ my own dreams

And I can't tell them no

Gonna be myself, nobody else

Gonna reach the sky if I only try

I can't wait to play
this for Mom!

I want this guitar so much! It's been at Dad's store for months and (luckily!) no one has bought it yet. Just imagine how amazing "Reach the Sky" (my song!) would sound if I was playing this guitar onstage at the Ryman! Maybe I can work at the store this summer or at Mom's food truck to earn the money to buy it!

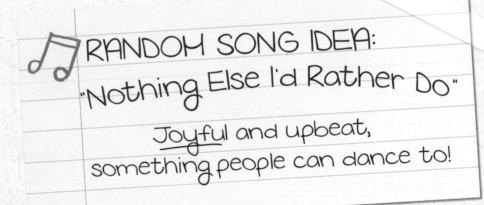

RANDOM SONG IDEA:
"Nothing Else I'd Rather Do"
Joyful and upbeat,
something people can dance to!

Tuesday, Octber 18th

I played "Reach the Sky" for Portia today, and she really helped me make it even better! But when I asked her to perform a duet with me at the Jamboree she turned me down. ☹ But then Portia told me why she's stopped playing music, and it's really sad. Turns out she had a stroke recently, and she's having trouble playing guitar now. I can't imagine how difficult it would be to not be able to play anymore. She must feel so discouraged. I wish there was something I could do to help her.

I also played my song for Mason. And he said "Reach the Sky" proves I'm a real songwriter. It felt so good to hear someone say that— especially Mason, since he never holds back if he doesn't like something! I feel like this is what I was born to do. I just want to write songs and perform for the rest of my life!

Friday, October 21st

Mason picked me up from school today with the best surprise ever!

He drove me and Jaya downtown so I could try out playing my song live. It sounded like a crazy idea at first, but downtown Nashville always has musicians playing on the sidewalks—who says I can't be one of them? Mason fixed up an amp for me as a surprise gift and Jaya painted it with flowers and my name. We found a good spot and set up. The amp looks amazing, and sounds even better. It felt so right to be playing my music for people and seeing them enjoy it. Performing makes me happier than anything else in the whole world!

WELCOME TO
NASHVILLE
TENNESSEE

Later . . .

Oh man. Mom and Dad were so mad that I performed without permission. Mason and I are both grounded. I tried to get them to see things from my point of view, but I feel like they aren't really listening to me. Maybe some kids wouldn't be ready for this, but I am. Writing songs and performing are the only things I'm 100% certain about. I know they want to protect me and for me to take things slow, but how can you go slowly when you're chasing the dream of your heart?

Song Idea:
"Can You Hear Me?"

Can you hear me? I'm talking to you.
Do you really see me? Or do you just
look through . . . me.
You say that you love me and you
want what's best,
But do you really know me? Are
you impressed?

I know what I want and I won't
back down.
I'm gonna follow my dreams. I hope
you'll come around.

So there.

Even later . . .

Wow. No wonder Mom's so protective of me. We had a really good talk tonight and Mom told me more about what happened to her when she was a young singer. She almost had a record deal, but her producer wanted to change her look and make her record other people's music. Then he stole her songs and told everyone she was difficult to work with so no one else would give her a chance. It sounds like a plot from a sad movie, right? So unfair!! Mom has one of the best voices I've ever heard! She should have been a star! I'm really glad she told me everything that happened to her. It makes me realize how important it is to stay true to yourself. I'm glad I have her on my team.

I love my parents so much. I know they always try to do what's best for me, even if I don't always understand it. Mom doesn't want me to get hurt like she was, but she also doesn't want to hold me back from my dreams. So . . . she and Dad are going to let me perform at the Bluebird after all!

I AM SO EXCITED!!! !!!

. . . And I have SO much practicing to do— I'm going to sing "Reach the Sky," so I need to make sure I can perform it perfectly!

Reach the Sky

intro: C G C G C G D F

C   G
I am planted in the ground

C   D
Tiny like a seed

C   D
Someday I will make you proud

     C G D G
I'll be steady like a tree

C   G   G
Will you teach me how to grow?

      C   G
Gonna be myself, nobody else

       D C G
Gonna reach the sky if I only try

I admit that I am young

Tucked beneath your wings

But someday I'll be on my own

Wild and flying free

Will you teach me how to sing?

Gonna be myself, nobody else

Gonna reach the sky if I only try

Am   C
I know you wanna keep me

    G   D
Safe away at home

Am   C
But I've got my own dreams

        C   G   C
And I can't tell them no

Gonna be myself, nobody else

Gonna reach the sky if I only try

Working on this song makes me think about all the reasons I love my parents—I just want them to be proud of me. I think this song's finally perfect! It's definitely the best song I've ever written!

Monday, October 24th

SOOOOO MEAN ←

Ugh. Know-It-All Holliday Hayes heard about the showcase and she told me I was dumb to think I'd get a record deal. She was so mean. She said, "You're Tenney Grant, not Taylor Swift. You're nothing special. I'm sure your music won't be, either." She's never even heard me play, but her dad does run a record label, so maybe she knows something I don't?

What if she's right? What if there's nothing special about my music and I'm the laughingstock of the showcase?

FRESH PICKED

RANDOM SONG IDEA:

Slow, sad song about Holliday judging me when she doesn't really know anything about my music!

Waylon always makes me feel better!

Saturday, November 5th

Today's the BIG day! In just 6 hours I will be on the stage at the Bluebird, playing my song. This morning, my parents surprised me with the aquamarine Taylor mini guitar I've been wanting for ages! It sounds so beautiful—I know it will help my song sound even better tonight when I play it!

Aubrey helped me with my outfit and makeup for the showcase and she gave me the prettiest comb for my hair that she made out of guitar picks. Who knew my little sister was such a fashionista?! My family is the best. I'd be way too nervous to perform tonight without them, so I'm so glad they'll be there to cheer me on. T-minus 5 hours and 54 minutes until I go onstage . . .

P.S. I've been practicing so much that my fingers are starting to have calluses on top of calluses!

How to Make a Guitar Pick Hair Clip
(Inspired by Aubrey Grant)

Grab a plain barrette or hair comb and a bunch of guitar picks.

Arrange the picks on the barrette in a fun design. Use glue dots to stick the guitar picks to hair clip, or use craft glue and let dry.

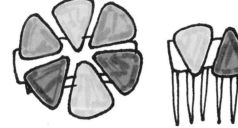

That's it!

Saturday, November 5th, 2 pm

It doesn't matter what I do—all I can think about is performing at the Bluebird later tonight. Time for a little pep talk in the form of lyrics . . .

(Untitled so far)

It's time to shine, it's time to sing
Fly, little bluebird, fly
Stretch your wings of melody
And carry my song up high

Fly, little bluebird, fly across the
    golden stage
Be yourself, nobody else. Leave
    behind your doubts and cage.

This line feels awkward. Come back to it later.

Not everyone will understand
Where your song comes from
But your words can show them
(Need line that rhymes with from)

Rethink this verse.

Fly, little bluebird, fly across the
golden stage
Be yourself, nobody else. Leave behind
    your doubts and cage.

The spotlight can feel harsh and bright
The pressure just too much high
But you are stronger than you feel
And you can reach the sky

Fly, little bluebird, fly across the golden stage
Be yourself, nobody else. Leave behind
    your doubts and cage.

Rhymes for "from": chum, come, drum, glum,
    some, slum, mum, hum
Rhymes for much: clutch, touch, hutch, such

Saturday, November 5th, 6 pm

We're here. I decided to take a minute to myself because journaling always calms me down. All of the other performers are at least ten years older than me and I am so nervous. The Bluebird Cafe is tiny. When I perform on a big stage, it's easy to focus because it's hard to really see everyone in the audience, especially with the spotlights on. But it's impossible NOT to see everyone in the audience here! I'm glad that I'll be able to see my family and Jaya and Portia, but not so glad to be able to see Holliday Hayes smirking at me. Yep, that's right—Holliday is here with her mom. And to think I had almost forgotten those mean things she said to me the other day . . .

T-minus 20 minutes until I go on . . . I know I'm supposed to play my best and be myself—but what if it isn't enough?

Beautiful

AWESOME

Tenney, you look amazing!!!
You are totally rocking this look and your
performance—you're a star! Mockingbird
Records would be crazy not to sign you!
I'm holding your journal while you perform
and I couldn't help but draw you. Sorry I
used up a songwriting page, Tens! Xo, Jaya

CRANK UP THE CONFIDENCE

MOCKINGBIRD RECORDS

Zane Cale
President & CEO
Mockingbird Records
260 Treble Square
Nashville, TN 37203

Saturday, November 5th, 9:54 pm

It wasn't enough.

I played really well—I know I did, I could feel it. But I did get flustered at the beginning and messed up just a little. Zane Cale liked my song and he thinks I have potential, but he said he felt like I didn't "own the stage" and that I'm not quite ready for a record deal.

I know I have a lot of time to make my dreams happen, and Zane thinks I'll be ready for a deal in a few years, but I feel like I failed.

I can't even face performing at the Jamboree. I feel so foolish for thinking I could have my big break at 12. ☹

Magnolia Hills Jamboree

Music

FOOD! FOLKS! FUN!

" Don't ask what the world needs. ASK WHAT MAKES YOU COME ALIVE, and go do it. Because what the world needs IS PEOPLE WHO HAVE COME ALIVE.**"**

—Howard Thurman

I just love the quote Jaya picked for the letterpress! Reminds me of how I feel when I'm playing!

Saturday, November 12th

The Jamboree was awesome—Holliday really did do a great job as committee chair. Never thought I'd hear myself say THAT!

I had decided not to perform, but guess who took my spot? Portia! It turns out that her stage name is Patty Burns—she's THE Patty Burns. Whaaaattt?!?!?! My mom has all of her records. I can't believe Portia wrote "April Springs." It's one of my all time favorite songs! Just thinking about it makes me want to sing it:

Last April the rains came down
And washed away your love
Last April the rains came down
And washed away my pride.
When I lost your heart in that rainstorm,
I think I nearly died

Portia asked me to perform with her, and I couldn't say no—I guess I should have known I wouldn't be able to stop performing for long. I played "Reach the Sky." Instead of being nervous and closing my eyes, I focused on the crowd and just had fun. Then we played "April Springs" together. That's what performing should always feel like—pure joy!

RANDOM SONG IDEA:

"Don't Let This Feeling Go"
Song about hanging on to the good moments in life to get you through the bad ones

Monday, November 14th
. . . .

OMG. Someone recorded my performance at the Jamboree and put it online. People everywhere are watching and hearing my song. It's so cool! It had over 15,000 views the last time I checked. Amazing! That's all I want—to share my music with the world!

And, even cooler, Zane saw my Jamboree performance and said it had everything that was missing at the Bluebird. He says I'm not quite ready for a record but . . .

He wants to be
MY MANAGER
and help develop
me as an artist!!!!

I want to just say YES!! of course, but I should probably think this through . . . It's a big decision! What if he wants to change me and my music like what happened to Mom? What if I really am too young? I want to talk it over with my parents and see what they think and make sure this is all okay with them. Will write more after dinner . . .

(Aubrey is obsessed with checking the views on the Jamboree video. I told her she could keep her list here.)

10:42 12,136 views

2:47   13,457 views

2:59   15,459 views

4:07   17,212 views

4:37   19,469 views

5:58   20,501 views

6:12   21,341 views

After dinner . . .

Mom and I talked for a long time and Mom said it was ultimately my decision if I wanted to work with Zane. I think I do, but I don't want to make a mistake!

Signing on with Zane as my manager:

Pros:

* Getting help with my songs to make them really great

* Maybe I'll get a record deal someday?!?

* I'll get better as a musician, singer, and songwriter

* Getting to meet famous Mockingbird musicians? ☺

* Taking my time to write songs that are totally me

Cons:

* Zane might work with me and then decide
  I'm not good enough for a record deal

* Busier schedule = less time with friends
  and family

* A lot of hard work for a long time!

* People might not take me seriously because
  I'm only 12

I've got a lot
to think about . . .

Mom and I just got back from meeting with Zane. I told him . . .

YES!!

So it's official:

I'M A
MOCKINGBIRD
SINGER SONGWRITER

This is the first big step to making my dreams come true, and it feels incredible!

Goals for Getting My Music Out There:

* Perform in public—anywhere and as much as I can! ✓

* Write a song that expresses who I really am ✓

* Perform at the Bluebird or another awesome venue ✓

* Get a manager ✓

* Sign a record deal! ✓

* Record my first album so I can share my music with the world! ✓

I think I need a new goals list. ☺ I want to remember this feeling forever!

CRANK UP THE CONFIDENCE

work **HARD** dream **BIG**

SHINE ON

I want to keep this feeling
For forever and a day
Carry it in my pocket
So it never goes away

Everyday I'm learning more and more
I'm finding out just who I am
I'll keep writing my songs
'Cause I know just where I stand

Need new line here that rhymes with "am"

I took the stage, nerves and all
I stood up in that spotlight
I didn't let my doubts get to me
And now I'm shining bright

Everyday I'm learning more and more
I'm finding out just who I am
I'll keep writing my songs

Need new line

'Cause I know just where I stand ←

Don't let anyone tell you that you
aren't special
Don't let anyone tell you that you
can't shine

I'm young and I've got lots to learn
But my friends have got my back
And my family knows me best
Their love's in every track

Everyday I'm learning more and more
I'm finding out just who I am
I'll keep writing my songs
'Cause I know just where I stand

Need new line

My schedule:

Sunday: Sunday Supper with the fam ☺

Monday: Work on some new songs with Portia

Tuesday: Help Dad at the store

Wednesday: More songwriting with Portia

Thursday: Help Mom with the hot chicken truck

Friday: Family movie night

Saturday: Practice guitar and banjo, work on some songs, "breakfast for dinner" sleepover with Jaya ☺

New schedule:

Sunday: Work on songs, help Mom with the food truck at the park, Sunday Supper

Monday: Work on new songs, run through finished songs at least twice

Tuesday: Prep new songs to play for Portia

Wednesday: Songwriting session with Portia

Thursday: Revise songs with notes from Portia

Friday: Songwriting session with Portia

Saturday: Morning banjo practice with Dad, sit in at Portia's recording session, sleepover at Jaya's

Saturday, March 4th

I got to sit in on Portia's recording session at Shake Rag Studios—it was so cool! I can't wait until it's my turn to record my first album (fingers crossed!). It's on days like this when I realize how lucky I am to live in Nashville. Music is this city's heart and soul. I can't think of anywhere else with so many recording studios and producers and musicians all in one place. It is <u>really</u> awesome.

So much music in those hands!

THOSE HANDS

One weird thing did happen at the studio. I got lost coming back from the bathroom and accidentally walked into the wrong recording studio and there was this boy playing the drums. He looked like he was about my age and he was kind of rude. I didn't know Zane worked with other young musicians. I'll have to ask Zane about him later . . .

Picky Pug

Prima Ballerina

Mr. Springy

Mr. Triangle

Jaya and I had some fun tracing around my guitar picks. We call them Pick People!

————————xxx————————

Saturday, March 4th, 10 pm

I'm sitting here in the dark in Jaya's room writing by the light of my phone. Jaya's already snoring—she ALWAYS falls asleep first at our sleepovers! But that's okay, it gives me a chance to write about our awesome new project in here!

So, Jaya's cousin Mina called from Bangladesh. A flood destroyed their school and they don't have the money to rebuild it. It's the only school for miles and miles (can you imagine that?!), and if it isn't fixed, Mina won't be able to go to school at all anymore. A few days off of school would be fun—sure—but how will Jaya's cousin keep learning with no school?

Jaya and I decided we should do something to raise money to fix the school. This is going to be fun—we'll help Mina and we'll get lots of time together. I've been missing my bestie—we haven't been able to hang out as much with all this music stuff going on. Now all we have to do is figure out how we're going to raise the money!

Ideas for Our Fund-raiser:

~~Jog-a-thon~~—too boring!

~~Sell a poster designed by Jaya~~—materials and printing too expensive ☹

~~Record a special song and sell copies~~—would take WAY too long

~~Bake sale~~—How much money could we really make selling muffins?

~~Benefit Concert~~—would need a BIG, star

Leroy Lion

Mr. Bear

Caitlin
the Cow

Clown Man

Monday, March 6th

Ugh. Miss Know-It-All Holliday Hayes overheard Jaya and me talking about our fund-raiser idea and she offered to help, which was nice of her, I guess. She is really organized and good at getting things done, but Holliday can also be really mean and bossy. Telling me that my music was nothing special a few weeks ago really hurt my feelings. And neither of us have forgotten how bossy Holliday was when she was in charge of the Jamboree. Why does she always have to act like she is so much better than everyone else?! It really bothers me that she's so rude when I've never been mean to her.

Of course, Jaya had my back. She told Holliday we'd let her know if we needed help once we had a plan. I love my bestie! But of course Holliday couldn't leave it at offering to help, she had to let us know we'd crash and burn without her. As if! Jaya and I make a fabulous team, and I know we'll figure out a great way to raise that money!

Lyrics brainstorm:

~~We're a pair and don't need a third~~
It's always been just her and me
We've no need for your thoughts
There no room for your bad energy
We're giving it our best shot

Some lyrics are easier to write than others. Can you imagine Holliday's face if I told her she inspired this song? Who knows—maybe it would inspire her to be a little nicer!

Tuesday, March 7th

I'm sitting here in the porch swing and the fireflies are out. Their blinking lights are kind of how I feel right now—excited and then not, worked up and then not. . .

I met with Zane and Portia today and played them some of the songs I've been working on. Zane liked most of them, but he and Portia both thought my new song should be faster and edgier. I'm going to really try my best to rework it, even if it does feel weird to me.

But I've got a lot of work to do! Zane reminded me that I need to have a full 30-minute set of songs so I can start booking gigs, and that my set needs to have a lot of different types of songs—they can't all be slow. 30 minutes of MY songs! Geez.

But the best part of my meeting was when Zane told me he was trying to book me to play at the Artists' Welcome Brunch before the City Music Festival. I'd be playing for some of the biggest musicians and label owners in town! That would be HUGE for me right now!

Songwriting Goals:

1. Work on songwriting every day
2. Practice every day
3. Work with Portia twice a week on my songs
4. Perform wherever and whenever I can
5. Finish my new song
6. Listen to all of the MP3s Zane gave me of great songs every singer-songwriter should know
7. Work with other musicians (and meet other Mockingbird stars!!!)

♫ RANDOM SONG IDEA:
"Workin' for the Dream"
Song with a driving beat about how you don't get what you want without working hard

From: Zane Cale
To: Tenney Grant
Subject: MP3s for you

Hello Tenney,

Here's the list of songs I was telling you about. Every singer-songwriter should know these great classics! MP3s are attached.

The Beatles—"I Want to Hold Your Hand"
The Isley Brothers—"Twist and Shout"
Stevie Nicks—"Landslide"
The Jackson 5—"ABC"
Bill Withers—"Ain't No Sunshine"
Patsy Cline—"Crazy"
Stevie Wonder—"I Believe (When I Fall in Love)"
Pat Benatar—"Hit Me With Your Best Shot"
Van Morrison—"Brown Eyed Girl"
The Beach Boys—"God Only Knows"
Aretha Franklin—"Respect"

Happy listening!
Zane

11 attachments

(Untitled song)

It was only going to be her and me
~~It's always been just her and me~~
~~We've no need for your thoughts~~ And then you
Planning   came in with
everything ~~There's no room for your energy~~ your thoughts
so perfectly
~~We're giving our best shot.~~
Giving your best shot

Chorus:

~~But you were there when I couldn't be~~

not loving   ~~And~~ I wish that ~~I was~~ could be ~~there now~~
all of this
Rework?   Where you are, where you are
Make
longer?   These words can only go so far

Go so far, go so far

↑ (need more for chorus here)

I thought I was the one
that could be there
I thought it would be me
Got a taste of life's dish of unfair
You showed me clarity
You are the one by her side
While I'm here on the sideline

Switch
these two
verses

Wednesday, March 8th

So. Jaya is my best friend, right? And we were going to do a fund-raiser for her cousin's school—it was going to be our thing.

Well, now Jaya has officially invited Holliday Hayes to help, too. How could she do that?! Holliday was so mean to me before my performance at the Bluebird. Jaya knows how hurt I was!

I like Jaya's idea for the fund-raiser—we're going to collect books and sell them at our school's Spring Clean. And I know Holliday will be a big help, but uuuggghhh!!! . . . I just wish it wasn't Holliday!!!

Book Drive To-Do List

- [ ] Find boxes for collecting books —▷ Tenney
- [ ] Set up collection boxes around town: school, music store, library, grocery, Senior Center —▷ everyone
- [ ] Design flyers —▷ Jaya
- [ ] Put flyers all around the neighborhood —▷ everyone
- [ ] Write and deliver morning announcement every Monday —▷ Holliday
- [ ] Pick up collection boxes —▷ Jaya and Holliday
- [ ] Sort and price books —▷ everyone
- [ ] Set-up booth to sell —▷ everyone
- [ ] Save the school in Bangladesh! ☺

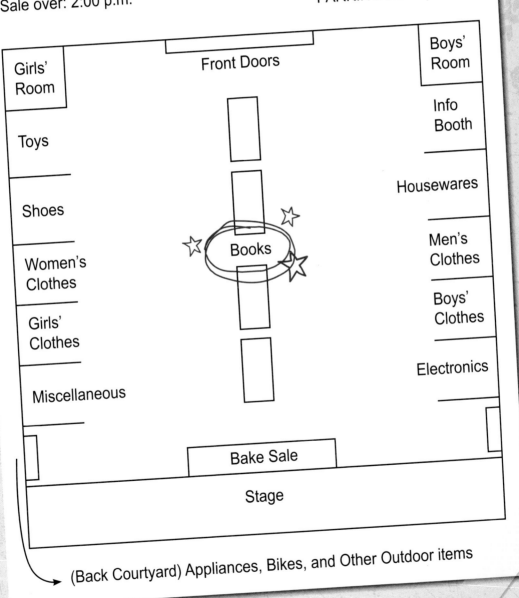

MAGNOLIA HILLS MIDDLE SCHOOL
SPRING CLEAN 2017

Gym open for setup: 9:00 a.m.
Doors open to public: 10:00 a.m.
Sale over: 2:00 p.m.

PARKING LOT

Boys' Room

Girls' Room

Front Doors

Info Booth

Toys

Housewares

Shoes

Books

Men's Clothes

Women's Clothes

Girls' Clothes

Boys' Clothes

Miscellaneous

Electronics

Bake Sale

Stage

(Back Courtyard) Appliances, Bikes, and Other Outdoor items

Songwriting Goals
CHECK-IN:

1. Work on songwriting every day
   So far, so good. I've only missed one day!

2. Practice every day ← So far, so good

3. Work with Portia twice a week on my songs ← So far, so good. _And drink Portia's sweet tea!_ ☺

4. Perform wherever and whenever I can
   Keeping my fingers crossed!

5. Finish my new song ← UGH, working on it

6. Listen to all of the MP3s Zane sent me of "great songs every singer-songwriter should know"
   → Working on it, but Aubrey keeps stealing my MP3 player because she loves all the songs so much!

7. Work with other musicians (and meet other Mockingbird stars!!!!) ← Maybe at the Artists' Brunch! yaaaayyyy!

Mom's voice in my head: "Do not use the stove or knives without me there to help!"

Recipe: Portia's Sweet Tea

Sprinkle 1/4 teaspoon of baking soda into a pitcher and add 12-15 tea bags (like Luzianne's or Lipton's; use more bags for stronger tea). Pour 4 cups of boiling water over tea bags and baking soda.

Cover and steep tea for 15-20 minutes. Remove tea bags and discard. Add 2 cups of sugar and stir until completely dissolved. Add 12 cups of cool water. Refrigerate until cold. Serve over ice with lemon slices.

The baking soda keeps the tea from being bitter!

REFRESHING

Thursday, March 9th

I'm sitting here waiting for Mom to pick me up from Shake Rag Studios, and if I was a cartoon character, there would be smoke coming out my ears! That drummer I walked in on the other day? His name is Logan Everett and HE IS SO ANNOYING!!! Zane wanted me to work with him on my new song. I didn't have much choice, so I gave it a shot. But we were working on _my_ song and he didn't listen to me AT ALL. If we were working on a song he wrote, I would have given my opinion but let him take the lead. I don't want to let Portia and Zane down, so I'm going to give him a chance, but I just don't think it makes any sense for us to work together!!

Mom's here, but note to self—

remember to fix
lyrics to new song with
what I improvised
in rehearsal.

Dreamer AND Doer

RANDOM SONG IDEA:
♫♪ "Not Yours"
With an angry driving beat.
About giving someone space
to do their own thing!

Thursday, March 9th, 6 pm

Logan sent me a bunch of songs to give me an idea about the direction he thinks we should take my song. Maybe his way of saying sorry for earlier?

Songs Logan Sent Me:

"At the Library" by Green Day
"4th of July" by Shooter Jennings
"Nashville Skyline Rag" by Bob Dylan
"Tough as Nails" by the Rusty Hammers
"Don't Slow Down" by Matt & Kim
"Don't Stop (Color On the Walls)" by
    Foster the People
"Miracle" by Paramore
"There You Go" by Johnny Cash
"You Ain't Going Nowhere" by the Byrds
"Lonely Boy" by the Black Keys
"Lonesome, On'ry and Mean" by Waylon Jennings
"Fell in Love with a Girl" by the White Stripes
"Rebel Hill" by Vinyl Thief
"Radio Silence" by the Black Cadillacs
"King of the Rodeo" by Kings of Leon

I sent him some back:

"Kodachrome" by Paul Simon
"Blue" by Joni Mitchell
"Teardrops On My Guitar" by Taylor Swift
"So Far Away" by Carole King
"April Come She Will" by Simon & Garfunkel
"Oklahoma Sky" by Miranda Lambert
"That's How You Know It's Love" by Deanna Carter
"Imagine" by John Lennon
"Headlights" by Dave Barnes
"Bluebird" by Sara Bareilles
"Dixieland Delight" by Alabama
"Boulder to Birmingham" by Emmylou Harris
"Say Anything" by Tristan Prettyman
"Carolina Highway" by the Tri-Stars

See? We have NOTHING in common.

Books for Bangladesh!

Your donations will help rebuild a school on the other side of the world!

Place your used books in the bins in the gym between now and the Spring Clean.

The money earned from the sale of the books will be sent to Bangladesh to help these girls rebuild their school.

For more information, contact Jaya Mitra, Tenney Grant, or Holliday Hayes.

Thank you for your donations!

Friday, March 10th

Okay, Logan sent me his version of my song. It's fast and rough and gravelly and it doesn't sound like I wrote it at all. But I was determined to think like a professional musician and did what Portia said. I really listened and gave it a chance. I played it with the drum track and just let myself sink into the music. And I have to admit, it was awesome. Playing it with a new tempo and the changes to the melody really brought out how I was feeling when I wrote it—not sad and ballad-y, but more angry and frustrated. It's weird how Portia and Zane and Logan could all see that the song needed those changes before I could, but I'm glad they said something about it. Because THIS is how I should feel when I play it—like everything inside is just bursting out. I can't wait for Monday's rehearsal!

Open your ears and really listen.
Really listening means hearing
somebody else's point of view.
Do that, and you won't just learn
about your song. You'll learn about
yourself, too.

—Portia

Monday, March 13th

I was kind of nervous to play through the new version of my song with Logan, but it actually went great! We listened to each other and tried some new things. The new chorus at the end is amazing—just what the song needed. I was wrong last week. This song really is a rock song and now I can't imagine it as anything else! Logan and I might not have anything in common, but that doesn't mean we can't work together if we both stay focused on the music.

On a scale of 1 to 10, I think today's jam session was an eleven!! Rocking out is pretty fun!

The only thing is . . .

. . . the Artists' Brunch is at the same time as the Magnolia Hills' Spring Clean. Between rehearsals and the performance, it turns out I won't be able to help much with the book drive and I'll miss most of the sale.

Jaya didn't say much when I told her, but I know she knows what a big deal this is for me. Plus, she's got Holliday to help her, and some other kids, too. I don't think she really needs me. I feel kind of bad about it, but it's the best I can do right now . . .

Sunday, March 11th

OMG these last few weeks have been crazy! How is it already only one week to the brunch (and Spring Clean)?! I've been trying to collect books for the fund-raiser between school and rehearsals and practicing and homework, but it's HARD. I'm so tired. I hope Jaya knows how much I really do want to be helping. Things haven't been quite the same since I told her I would only be there for the end of the Spring Clean. And Holliday being around so much isn't helping! Jaya and I were a pair, and now I just feel like a third wheel. I miss my best friend. I miss US.

The Nashville City Music Festival

cordially invites you
to attend the

Artists' Welcome Brunch

April 8th
10 a.m. - 1 p.m.

1618 Harding Way
Nashville, TN 37205

Includes live entertainment from
some of Nashville's (rising stars!)

Kindly RSVP to
mike@citymusicfestival.com by March 21st

That's me!
(and Logan)

Only 3 days until
the brunch! Eek!

Saturday, April 8th, 7 am

Today is the Artists' Brunch!!! I am so excited and so nervous and so jittery. In just a few hours, the people I listen to on the radio are going to be listening to _me_ and _my_ songs. It almost doesn't feel real. Then Dad and I have to hustle over to the book sale. It's going to be a seriously busy day!

Ways NOT to Be Nervous:

* Take lots of deep breaths before I go onstage

* Close my eyes and picture everyone in the audience wearing funny glasses

* Pretend I'm performing for Jaya and my friends at school instead of BIG STARS!

* Pick a spot on the wall over everyone's heads and look at that while I perform

Who am I kidding?! I'm going to be nervous no matter what! I just need to channel that energy into my music. Wish me luck!

RANDOM SONG IDEA:
"Not Gonna Get to Me"
Song about pushing
through when you're
scared or nervous about
something

Song Idea #2: "Flow Through Me"
Slow, lyrical, calming song about
trusting that things will go fine

City Music Festival
Artists' Brunch Set List

— ○ ○ ○ —

"Where You Are" by Tenney (and Logan)

"Home Again" by Tenney

"Drive My Car" by the Beatles

"Carolina Highway"
   by Ray and Georgia Grant

"I Walk the Line" by Johnny Cash

"Reach the Sky" by Tenney

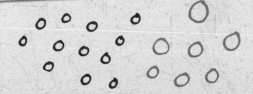

Saturday, April 8th, 1:34 pm

I'm so confused. Today has felt like a roller coaster. I was so nervous performing at the brunch (and our first song was a little rocky!), but then Logan and I got into a groove and played really well. It was so exhilarating playing live for such a big audience, and it just made me feel like I was floating on air. Everyone wanted to talk to us and congratulate us—I felt like a real star.

But then Logan had to be such a jerk! He acted like he saved our set when we BOTH messed up a tiny bit. He doesn't even write original songs—if it wasn't for playing with me, he wouldn't have been invited to play at all. Ugh! He's so full of himself!

I got to talk about music with Belle Starr.

BELLE STARR!!

I know I said before that her music isn't my thing, but come on—BELLE STARR!! And she gave me her business card and wrote her personal e-mail on it and told me to e-mail her anytime! (I can't believe she's kind of sort of my friend now! Aubrey is going to freak out!)

Belle gave me some really great advice about music, but she also told me that it's important to keep my friends as close to my heart as my music. She said sharing your music and success with your friends makes everything in life better. I'm lucky to have my family and friends like Jaya to share things with!

But then I stayed too long at the brunch. We're in the car now zooming to the book sale, but—who am I kidding?—it's already over. I hope Jaya isn't too mad at me.

belle@bellestarrmusic.com

DO <u>NOT</u> LOSE THIS!

Roller Coaster

Up and down, spin me round and round
Like a roller coaster in my head
I'm high then low, fast then slow
Until I crash-land on my bed

I'm chasing my dreams
Yeah, it means everything
And I'll never give up
Even when things get tough
'Cause my dreams mean everything

ROLLER COASTER

Saturday, April 8th, 6:12 pm

Jaya and I have never had a fight like this before. I know I've been busy with my music, but I can't believe she thinks I'm not a good friend. I'm sad, and I'm kind of angry, too. She's giving me such a hard time about choosing the brunch over the book sale. This is my dream. I thought she understood. I thought she was my biggest fan.

I feel awful. My music is so, so important to me, but so is Jaya. I think she's wrong about me, but that doesn't make me feel any better.

Monday, April 10th

It's Monday after the brunch and here I am eating alone at lunchtime. I feel like I should be mad at Jaya for sitting with Holliday instead of me, but really I'm just sad. I wouldn't even be where I am with my music if Jaya hadn't encouraged me when I first started playing . . . Does she know that?

Wouldn't be here without you . . .
Only me because you encourage me . . .
Push me to do my best, be my best . . .
Wouldn't have courage to follow my dreams . . .
Taught me what it means to be a good friend . . .

Sing from my heart / Jaya in my heart . . .
When I play, you're there with me . . .

Lyrics Brainstorm:

~~You push me to be my best~~ You put your life in my dreams

~~Comfort me when I want to scream~~

~~I have you and I'm so blessed~~ And help things go right behind the scenes

~~You give me the strength~~ You mean so much to me

And I hope you see

~~When I'm up there on the stage~~

Every time I play

You're the music, you're the music

         word

In every ~~song~~ I sing

You're the music, you're the music

You are the music in me

When I look at the crowd

Your smiling face stands out

You taught me this is what life's all about

So I hope I make you proud

Monday, April 10th, 7:23 pm

Well, I never thought I'd say this, but Holliday Hayes just saved the day. (I know, right? Crazy!) I decided to swallow my pride and talked to her about my fight with Jaya. She actually helped me understand where Jaya was coming from. She told me Jaya wasn't that upset about not raising enough money—that she was more upset I wasn't there to work on it with her. I really let Jaya down. Then Holliday apologized for sort of taking over the book drive and making me feel like they didn't need me. It was the first time I've ever had a conversation with Holliday that felt real. I can see why Jaya likes her.

I feel like we might actually be starting to become friends, which is really cool.

Together, Holliday and I decided to put on a benefit concert to raise the rest of the money to save Mina's school. I really want to show Jaya how much her friendship means to me, and that I care about the things she cares about because she's my best friend. I just hope we can pull it off!

P.S. "Star Like Me" is totally back in my head on repeat. Although, after meeting Belle and finding out how cool and nice she is, I don't think I mind. ☺

11:14 pm
I've been trying to fall asleep for more than an hour, but my brain won't turn off! I just keep rehearsing in my head what I'm going to say to Jaya when I tell her tomorrow morning about our idea for the benefit concert. Why am I more nervous about this than I was even for the brunch?

Tuesday, April 11th

So I talked to Jaya this morning and we both apologized. She was as miserable as I was about our fight! She's excited about working on the concert together (with Holliday, too, of course!)—and this time, there's no way I'm letting anything distract me!

Dreamer AND Doer

Benefit Concert for Bangladesh School!

Saturday, 1 p.m.

Grant's Music and Collectibles, East Nashville

$15 at the door

With special guest,
country music legend Patty Burns!

Benefit To-Do List:

☐ Reorganize Dad's store to make room for
   a stage and guests

☑ ~~Flyers? Announcements? Posters?~~ *Done! Jaya*
   ~~We need to get the word out~~ *made us the*
   ~~about the show!~~ *coolest flyers!*

☐ Print 100 tickets

☐ Book acts to play—Portia? The Tri-Stars?
   Dad's friend Joe?

☐ E-mail Belle Starr to ask her to play as
   the headliner

☐ Figure out my set list

☐ Finish song for Jaya and rethink end to
   "Where You Are"

☐ Banner for the show

~~☐ Lights~~ Dad and Mason will take care of this!

~~☐ Microphones and sound system set-up~~ *same*

☐ Ask food trucks to come for outside the
   show? Mom's Hot Chicken (obviously!!).
   R & Brie Grill? Peace, Love, and Biscuits?
   Pho Sho? Sugar Rush Ice Cream?

☐ Folding Chairs—125

There is so much to do! I hope we didn't bite off more than we can chew! I'm a little nervous—I want it to be perfect so Jaya can see how much her friendship means to me. Will it be enough?

P.S. Zane sent this photo he took of me and Logan at the brunch. We do look like we're having fun, I guess, even though we messed up "Where You Are." I know I don't ever have to play with him again, but I do kind of regret those things I said. And if I'm being honest, it's kind of weird to think about performing without him at the benefit concert.

Where You Are

I thought I was the one who should be there

I thought it would be me

Got a taste of life's dish of unfair

You showed me clarity

You are the one by her side

While I'm here on the sideline

Chorus:

I wish that I could be

Where you are, where you are

These words can only go

Go so far, go so far

I see you've got it under control

Just wish I could be the other hand to hold

I wish that I could be

Where you are, where you are

It was only going to be her and me

And then you came in with your thoughts

Planning everything so perfectly

Giving your best shot

Now while I'm over here alone

You're making sure she isn't on her own

I wish that I could be

Where you are, where you are

These words can only go

Go so far, go so far

I see you've got it under control

Just wish I could be the other hand to hold

I wish that I could be

Where you are, where you are

Bridge:

I've been so out of touch lately

Been caught up with myself

Been taking out my anger on somebody else

I'm so sorry

I know you don't mean me any harm

You're just being a good, good friend

Making light of the dark

I just want to be

Where you are, where you are

These words can only go

Go so far, go so far

So now we have worked it all out

Thank you for erasing my doubt

I just want to be

Where you are, where you are

My Set List for the Benefit Concert

(and Logan's!)*

"Reach the Sky" by Tenney

~~"Home Again" by Tenney~~

~~"Drive My Car" by the Beatles~~

"Where You Are" by Tenney and Logan

"Music in Me/Jaya's Song" by Tenney

"I Walk the Line" by Johnny Cash

"Magnolia Midnight" by Zane

✻ I apologized to Logan. We're both still learning that being a musician is about more than just singing or playing your instrument—you have to know how to work as a team, too. He agreed to play at the benefit concert. I hate to admit it, but I feel much better knowing I'll have a partner up there . . .

(But after this, we're both back to being solo acts!)

Music in Me

by Tenney Grant
Dedicated to Jaya Mitra

You put your life in my dreams
And help things go right behind
    the scenes
You mean so much to me
And I hope you see

Chorus:
That every time I play
You're the music, you're the music
In every word I sing
You're the music, you're the music
You are the music in me

When I look at the crowd
Your smiling face stands out

You taught me this is what life's all about
So I hope I make you proud

'Cause every time I play,
You're the music, you're the music
In every word I sing
You're the music, you're the music
You are the music in me

Bridge:
You'll be by my side
So don't be afraid
I'd rather say I tried
Than let this dream fade

Every time I play,
You're the music, you're the music
In every word I sing,
You're the music, you're the music
You are the music in me

Jaya's Songbirds for the World

1. Draw or trace a bird shape and cut it out to make a stencil.

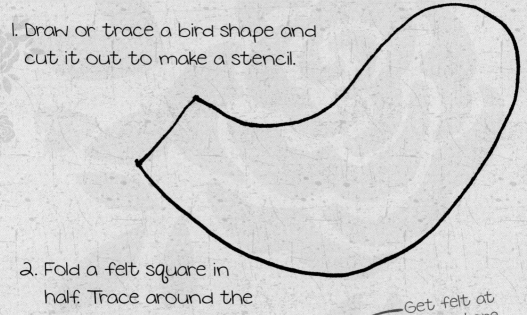

2. Fold a felt square in half. Trace around the bird stencil, and then holding the two pieces of felt together, cut out the two birds at once.

Get felt at craft store.

3. Cut out two wings and a beak from a different color felt.

4. Use craft glue to attach the beak and a loop of string or ribbon.

Part of a tissue or a cotton ball works!

Pinch around edges to make sure it stays together!

5. Put some stuffing in the middle and craft glue around edges, and then stick second bird shape on top.

6. Glue wings on the sides. Add a bead or circle of felt for an eye on each side. Let dry!

Hang your bird wherever you need a song!

Jaya made these songbirds in colors of flags from around the world!

Bangladesh

Brazil

United States

Germany

Saturday, April 22nd

Aaaaaahhhh! It's here!

The benefit concert is TODAY! I have a good feeling about this—everything seems to have fallen into place.

Hmmmmmm . . . smells like Mom is making her apple doughnuts—the quickest way to get me, Aubrey, and Mason (and Dad!) out of bed. Better go get some while they're hot. ☺

12 pm
Only 1 hour until the show! I shouldn't be
writing in here—there's too much to do—
but I had to write this down because I
can hardly believe it's real . . . ⟶ ⟶ ⟶

Belle Starr told her millions of followers about our show! The concert is going to be crazy!!! (in a good way!!!!)

BelleStarr

Sad I won't be able to make a great show today @ 1 p.m. at <u>Grant's Music and Collectibles</u> in East Nashville.

Please go show your support for Patty Burns, Logan Everett, and my friend Tenney Grant! She's a star on the rise.

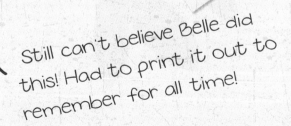

Still can't believe Belle did this! Had to print it out to remember for all time!

Saturday, April 22nd 8:14 pm

Soooo . . . over 300 people showed up to our benefit concert! It was great to sing with Portia, and Logan and I finally played together like a real duo. We sounded pretty awesome, if I do say so myself. ☺

Plus, Jaya loved the song I wrote for her, and we raised more money than we needed—which means Jaya's cousin and her friends will get their school back!

RANDOM SONG IDEA: "This is How It Feels" Triumphant song, with a beat people can dance for joy to!

"Breakfast for Dinner"
Blueberry Muffins

Prepare a box of blueberry muffin mix according to the directions on the box. I always add in 2 tablespoons of lemon zest for a special homemade touch!

In another bowl, mix together 2 tablespoons of melted butter, 2 tablespoons of flour, 2 tablespoons of light brown sugar, and 1/4 cup of raw sugar to make sugar topping.

Fill muffin cups about 3/4 full of batter. Sprinkle each cup of batter with about 1 tablespoon of topping. Bake according to the directions on the box. Serve warm.

(Yes, Mom, I know—never use the oven without you around. ☺)

THE BEST SLEEPOVER FOOD

Agreed! (Sorry for writing in your notebook, Tens . . . I just love these muffins so much!)

xo, Jaya

I could get used to this breakfast-for-dinner tradition! Thanks for having me over, Tenney.

♡ Holliday

Tuesday, May 2nd

I can't believe how much has happened this year. I feel so lucky. Sometimes I have to pinch myself to make sure it's all really real!

* I played a showcase at the Bluebird Cafe.

* Zane Cale from Mockingbird Records signed on to be my manager.

* Portia "Patty" Burns, songwriting legend, is helping me with my songwriting.

* I played with Portia at the Jamboree.

* A video of me singing my original song went viral online.

* I have a new writing partner in Logan Everett.

* I learned I can write all different kinds of songs and my songwriting is getting stronger every day.

* Logan and I played the Artists' Brunch and got to meet some of the biggest names in music.

* I met Belle Starr and we're sort of friends now.

* I made a new friend in Holliday Hayes.

* Jaya, Holliday, and I raised enough money to help rebuild Jaya's cousin's school.

* And TODAY . . .

ZANE SIGNED LOGAN AND ME TO A RECORDING CONTRACT!!!!

I'll admit it, I had to think for a moment before I signed on the line. I always pictured myself recording my first album as a solo act, but Zane wants Logan and me to record an album in a couple of years as a duo.

Yeah, I'm worried it's going to be really tough for Logan and me to work together writing (and rewriting many times I'm sure) enough songs for a whole album. But working with other people is part of being a musician, and Logan and I did play really well together at the benefit. We can make it work! How could I say no to this once-in-a-lifetime opportunity?!

HAPPY DANCE!

New Goals:

1. Write enough songs to record my first album—10? 12? I'll have to ask Ellie and Zane.

2. Get to know Holliday even better since I think we're going to be good friends.

3. Get comfortable enough playing the banjo to use it in performances from time to time—I'm getting close!

4. Work with Logan on new songs to make sure our sound varies from song to song.

5. Make plenty of time for Jaya and my family—it can't be all music all the time!

6. Book some more small performances so I can get really comfortable onstage.

7. Have fun!

————————————— ×××——————————————

Friday, May 5th

Well, I'm all out of pages. I guess it's time
to get a new journal to fill with more
songs and more of my story.

Blank pages are calling my name
Melodies swirling 'round in my brain
Write 'em down and then give 'em a try
Can't stop me—I'm gonna fly!

P.S. Jaya says she can't get "Music in Me" out
of her head. I apologized, but she said having
my music in her head is like getting to hang
out with me all the time. (AWWW!) But I'm sure
she'll get over that soon since she'll be listening
to me practice A LOT! Maybe I should buy her
a tambourine for her birthday so she can jam
along with me! ☺ Because the only thing
better than playing music is playing it with the
people I love most!

♡ Tenney